MW00910411

Come join Prune, Prosper and Fido.
To follow them in their adventure,
unfold the pull-out picture.

Investigate With Prune and Prosper

At the Zoo

BARRON'S
New York • London • Toronto • Sydney

It is Wednesday.
Since it's such a nice day,
Prune, Prosper and Fido
have come to say hello to the animals.
But everyone at the zoo is excited—
a flying saucer has landed
and some strange animals have come out of it.
"These must be the Sillikins!" says Prune.
"They must have left their own planet to colonize our zoo.
But we're going to find them."

Easier said than done! The Sillikin is a joker
and can change its appearance.
It takes advantage of this by playing mean tricks!
But one little thing always gives it away.
When you recognize it, it asks a question.
If you answer correctly, it returns to its normal form
and becomes as well-behaved as can be.
But, if you make a mistake, Pfft! It disappears again.
The monkeys saw four Sillikins go by. They were talking
to the guard, and going toward the elephant house.
"With the guard? Hmm, that's strange," says Prosper.
"Prune, Fido, come on, we have to find them
before they turn the whole zoo upside down."

 **Do you see the elephant house?**

"Prosper, look! I would bet three peanuts that one of the Sillikins is there. He has changed his shape!"

Do you see the Sillikin inside the elephant house?

"Sillikin, we've seen you, come here!"
"La-dee-dah!" Says the Sillikin. "If you want to catch me, you have to look hard. Thanks to me, one of the baby kangaroos has left his pouch."

Can you help find the baby kangaroo?
(He's not far away from his mother.)

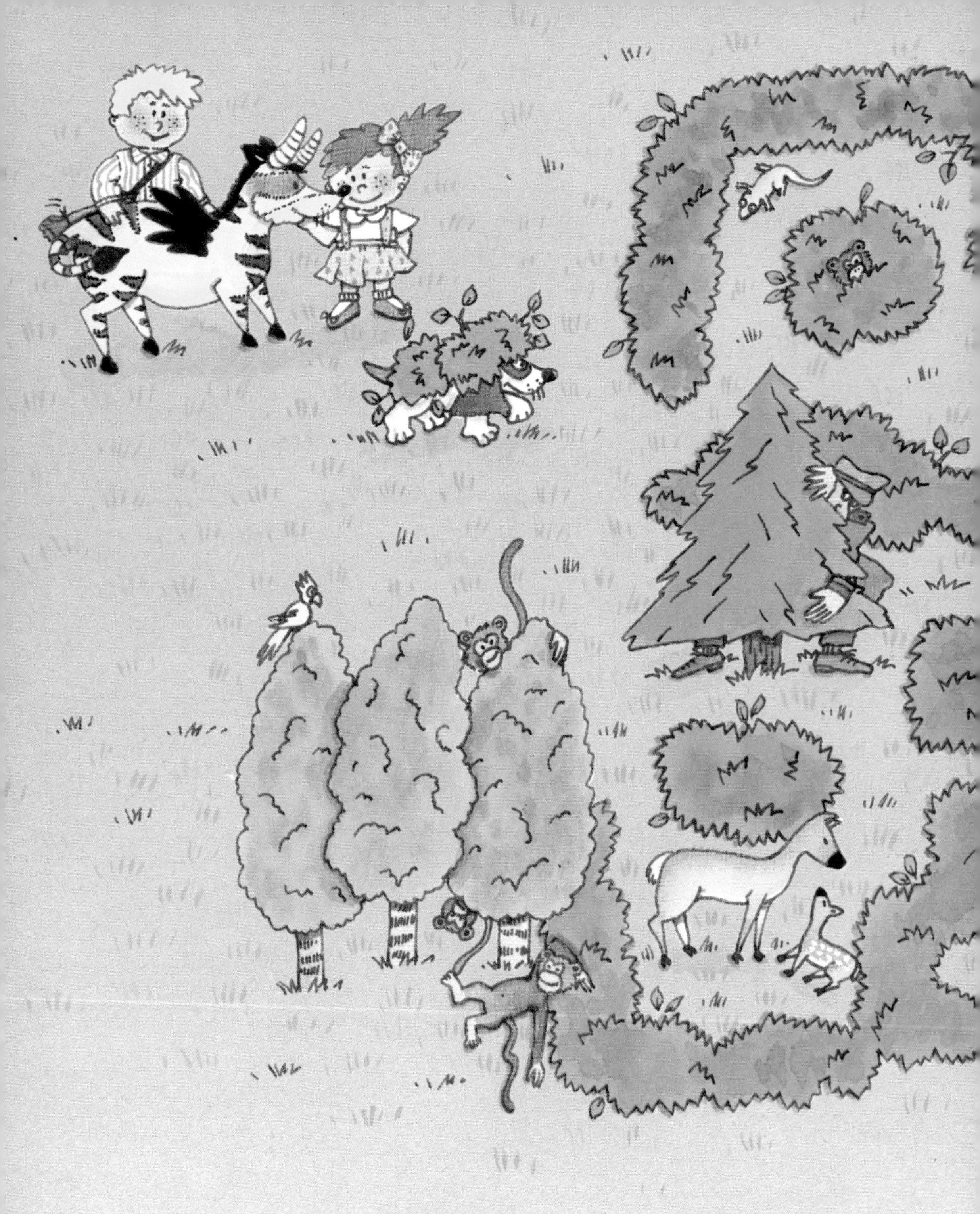

To return to the flying saucer, Prune, Prosper, Fido and the first Sillikin must go through the deer and wild boar enclosure.

Do you see where it is?

"Prune, look, the guard! He mustn't see us.
If he is helping the Sillikins, he'll keep us from going through!"

Can you help our friends get through the maze without being seen?"

Now, we have to find the other Sillikins.
Let's go look around the reptile house.
"Hello, crocodiles. Greetings, Mrs. Python."
Prune and Prosper are so busy greeting their friends
that they haven't yet noticed the second Sillikin
which has melted into the background.

But you see it, don't you?

"Sillikin, there you are! Come with us to your saucer!"
"La-dee-dah!" says the Sillikin. "If you want to catch me, you really have to search. Thanks to me, one of the lizards has escaped from the reptile house."

Do you see where it is hiding?

The guard is barring the door. Will our friends be trapped?
"Come this way!" says Mother Python. "There's a secret exit."

"But before leaving, help me. My 19 babies must go to bed, but since they are all tangled up, I can't count them."

Can you tell if all the babies are really there?
(Careful, don't count the boa constrictor in the tree!)

What a show at the monkey house! They are playing and pulling at each other. Prune and Prosper love to watch them. Suddenly, Prune says, "Prosper, look—the third Sillikin is here!"

Can you find this Sillikin?
(It's watching the monkeys, too.)

"Sillikin, you're ours. You'd better come quietly!"
"La-dee-dah!" says the Sillikin. "If you want to catch me, you really have to search. Thanks to me, one of the monkeys is pretending to be a frog in the hippo enclosure."

 **Do you see it?**

"Let's take this prisoner to the saucer quickly!" says Prosper.
"Look, there, behind the hippo!" says Prune,
as she stares at a torn picture lying on the ground.
What is Prune so afraid of?

To find out, imagine that all the pieces of the torn pictures have been put back together.

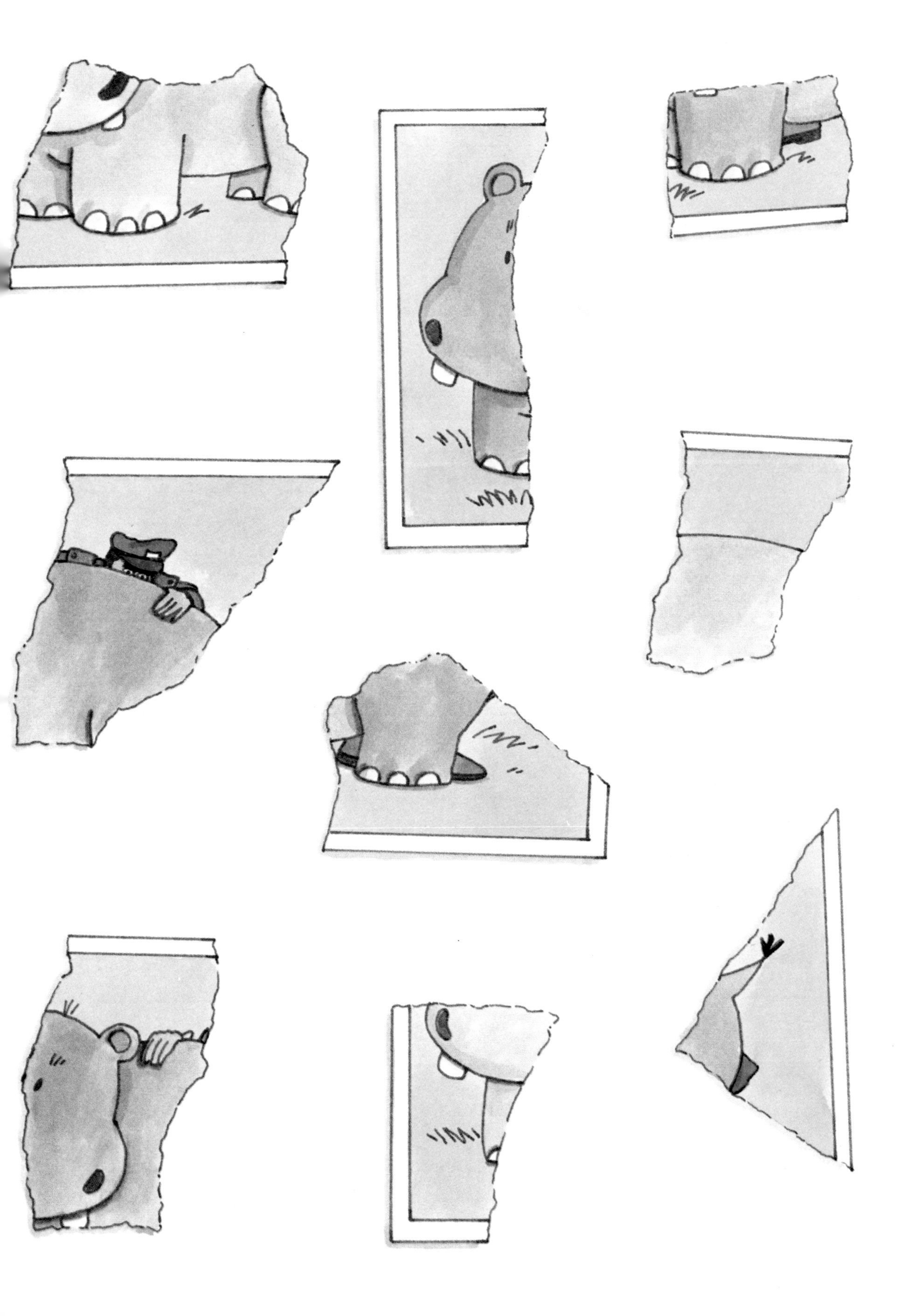

The giraffes have invited their friends
to celebrate their children's birthday.
"I see the fourth Sillikin," shouts Prosper.
He's changed himself into a baby animal, but something is
wrong with his legs!"

Can you find the fourth Sillikin?

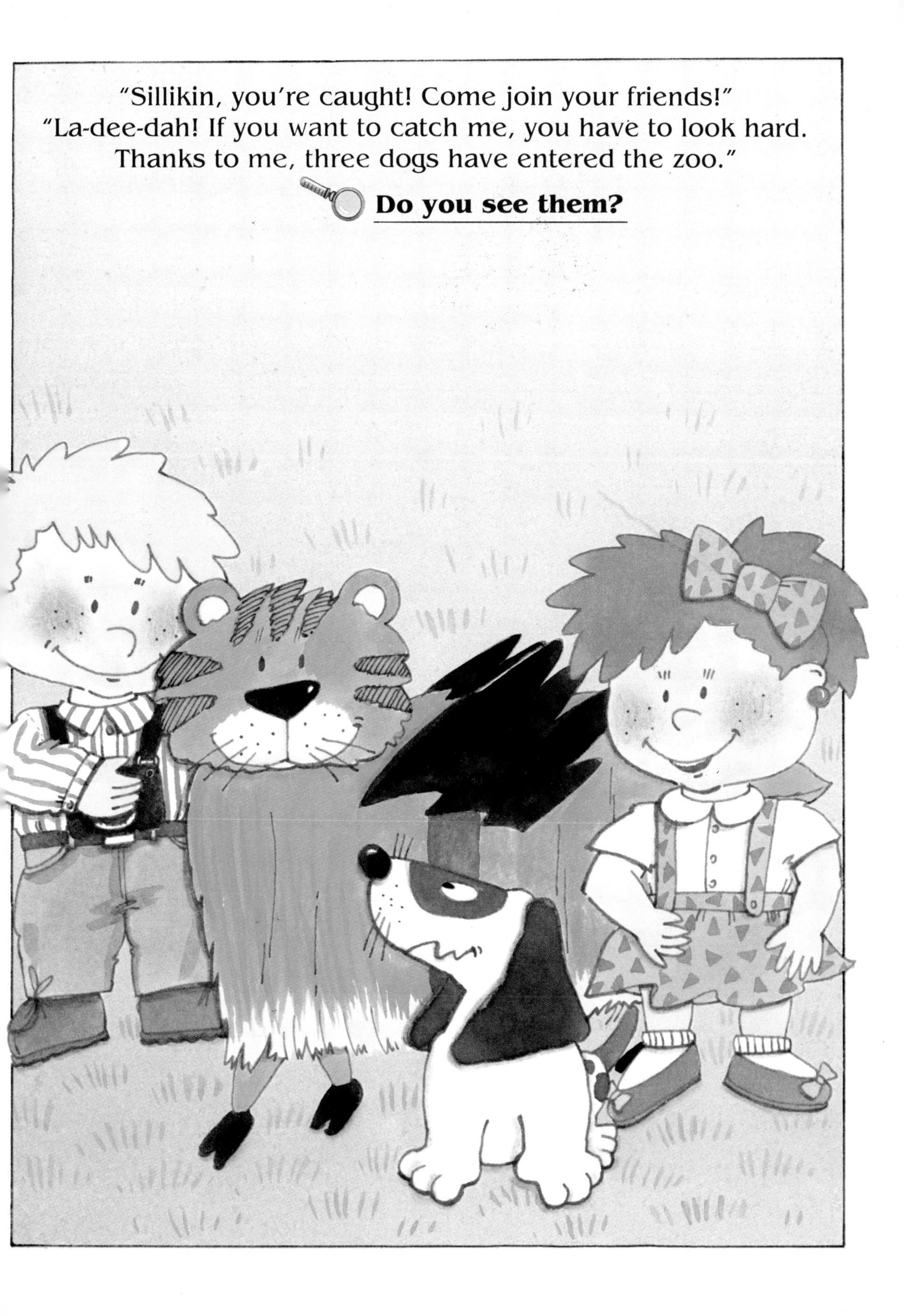
"Sillikin, you're caught! Come join your friends!"
"La-dee-dah! If you want to catch me, you have to look hard.
Thanks to me, three dogs have entered the zoo."
Do you see them?

Prune, Prosper and Fido take the last Sillikin to the saucer.
But suddenly while passing the refreshment stand . . .

(Do you see where it is?)

The guard appears! "Halt! Let him go at once!" he says.
No! This is too much! Before he knows what is happening,
our friends have captured the mean guard, too.

"Let's shut him up in the shed!" says Prune.

Can you count the guard's keys?

"Goodness!" exclaims Prosper. "The real guard is there—tied up!"
"But, then . . . the one we have, who is he?"

Can you find the one clue that will give you the answer?

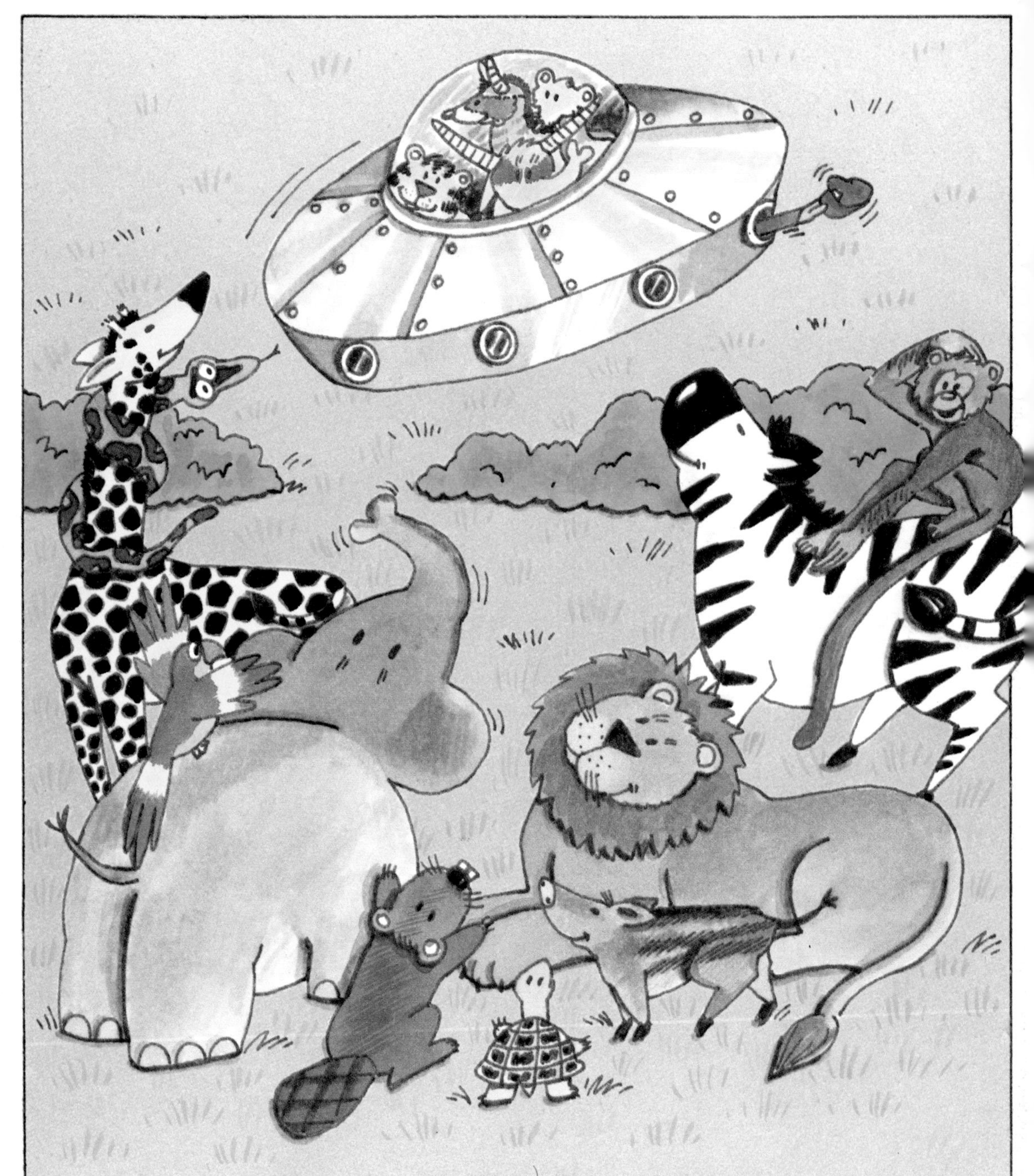

The fake guard is also a Sillikin!

But all's well that ends well, thanks to Prune and Prosper.
Those tricky Sillikins have left,
after promising to behave when they return.
"In that case, have a good trip, and come back soon!"
say the animals in the zoo.